A TALE OF FRIENDS, ENEMIES AND MINECRAFT

BY: JAKE MAYER

Chapter 1

One day, a hot humid summer day, August 24th to be exact, Mike Craft, also known as Captain Craft was busy as normal playing Minecraft. That is why he was called "Captain Craft" by his gaming friends. Minecraft is a video game that lets the player walk around in a universe made of blocks. The player collects certain blocks that let him do specific things. You can combine blocks that you have collected to make new things. It is a great game for creative kids that like engineering and like to make new cool awesome stuff. That was perfect for Mike. He was a 10 year old computer genius that just knew he was going to be famous someday. He thought it would be because he developed some amazing new technological invention. This story is about exactly how he went about getting famous and how he developed his technology.

So that day, he was just moving normally around in his world, picking up blocks in order to build a house, when for no reason a pig began to walk around in his house. The pig was just straight out annoying. This made him realize he was getting low on food and he should get some pork chops. He also realized that he was getting very bored playing Minecraft alone. He remembered he had permission to log on to his friend's personal multi player server. After a brief moment when he could not remember his friend's directions, he was able to log on to his friend's server.

His friend's name was Mark Jebson. They have been best friends since pre-K. They met on the red and blue carpet where the building blocks were kept. They both loved to build so they immediately became friends. They grew up building Legos and when Minecraft come out, they both fell in love with it. They spend as much time as they can playing either the single player game by themselves or playing together now that Mark has put a server on his Mac.

As he was figuring out where he spawned in the server world he quickly saw his friend in the game. Mike was still building his house because he was new to the server. He had visions of it looking like a mansion but so far it looked more like a hut. There was plenty of time to fix that because Mark had agreed to help him. They were both having fun playing with the stuff that Mark had built on the server before Mike joined. Mark had made a roller coaster, a water ride and a weird piston clock that he still could not figure out. He also liked being the only one on the server besides his friend because there was not a chance that he could be griefed when he built something cool like Mark's piston clock. That day he decided to ask Mark to help him finish his house. Together they built an amazing structure that looked a lot like Bill Gate's house. They used mainly brick blocks with many other types for decoration. They also made amazing chandeliers with glow stone blocks, glass blocks and fences. They were stoked with the results. When he finished his house he went on to lay the boundaries for more houses for when new friends joined the server. But it would be a while before more people got on his server because they just weren't ready to give up their private world.

The one thing that did make him mad was that the server was almost never up! Mark rarely had his server turned on because he only wanted it turned on when he was on. Mike eagerly accepted any chance he had to go on the server because he did have fun whenever he could play in Mark's game.

That steamy afternoon when they just accomplished so much on Mark's server there was a problem. All of the sudden the computer froze up. It felt like the end of the world to Mike. He feared that he had just lost his beautiful creation. But no worry, Mark's server backs itself up once a minute and all they lost was one boundary wall. So upon investigating what the heck was going on, Mike found out that his little sister was playing with the modem and unplugged the Ethernet cable. In his investigation, Mike did not know how the cables got unplugged so he first asked his mom what was the problem or if she turned it off. She said she did not so he looked further and he went to the cable room he saw his sister unplugging cords.

Chapter 2

His sister's name is Lilly and she was totally a pain in Mike's neck because she was three years old and his parent's favorite. They let her do anything she wanted and she never got in trouble. Like the time she put a peanut butter and jelly sandwich on his tri fold for the science fair that he spent 5 hours on and she destroyed it. They did not even yell at her. They just said to her in a sweet tone of voice, "That is ok, just do not do it again,". She was like a real life creeper (a Minecraft villain) or worse. That really made Mike mad because he had to do it all over again. He was very mad that he had to do it all over again. But he did do it again and it was better than before! He changed the fonts and added more pictures which made it clearer. His teacher said it really showed what he was trying to demonstrate and she gave him an A! He did not feel he should thank his little sister though.

After a little bit of re-engineering the cable room, he reattached the loose cables and locked the door when he was done to make sure his sister could not do it again. It took him a minute to rejoin the game because the Wifi took a while to reboot. When it rebooted he looked at the server and it was down. Mark had thought Mike had quit for the day when he got disconnected so he shot it down. He called Mark and asked politely to speak to him because Mark's mom had answered. Mark came on the phone laughing because his sister just told him a joke. Mark was happy to turn back on the server and they both started to get back into the game.

He had just decided to make a train station in that huge house that he and Mark had made, when his mom, also known as Julie Craft, came and said he should play outside. Captain Craft was not very happy but he thought quickly and decided to ask Mark to play basketball. Mike figured that while he was playing basketball he would also be able to talk about Minecraft. His friend loved basketball more than Mike did so he knew that he would say yes. They met each other at the town park where they had several courts to play on. There was one vacant one that they could play by themselves. Mike did score a basket once but then two seconds later Mark scored a basket. They kept on playing until they got picked up an hour later by Mike's dad also known as Jason Craft. He actually sort of enjoyed himself and gave his mom some credit for having a good idea.

When he got home, he was dying to play Minecraft, but his mom tried to stop him by telling him that he played too much. "How could she think that? I just spent an hour playing basketball!" He refused to be deterred. He negotiated another hour on his computer with his mom by saying he would not play Minecraft. Instead he would watch tutorial videos so he could learn new engineering techniques and build new inventions in his Minecraft world. She thought that sounded good and that he may as well learn something instead of just play a video game.

He started watching a tutorial video on the piston clock that Mark had made and realized he could do it too. After that video he watched a Youtube video on how to make red stone machines smaller and more efficient. In Minecraft, red stone is the equivalent of electrical wiring. You have to find and mine red stone just like all of the other metal and stone blocks. Switches allow you to turn on and off the red stone and control its effects. Knowing how to use red stone is essential for making machines in Minecraft. Making creations with red stone was super interesting to

Mike because he is very interested in computers and making red stone machines is a lot like building a computer. As he was searching Youtube, he ran across a series of videos on red stone creations. He was very excited about them because this series of videos had many cool machines that actually worked. Because of these and the video he watched earlier, he began to make plans in his head how to make very small, very useful red stone machines. Red stone machines can take up a lot of space if you make them inefficiently. So making them smaller would make them more efficient and easier to use inside buildings. That way you don't have to make separate rooms full of red stone to power your machines. Or you don't have to make a basement for your house just for red stone. This was going to be very helpful if he was going to add red stone machines to his house. He could not wait to tell Mark how to make a mini red stone machine.

..s small machine was going to be a huge success for their multi player server. He spent the rest of the night imagining new red stone machines and how they would work together to make even more amazing things. He fell asleep in front of his Mac dreaming about crazy new inventions that he would make the next day in Minecraft. This was the germ of the idea that would lead to his success.

Chapter 3

He woke up with a smile on his face because of his sweet Minecraft dreams. But the smile changed when Mike realized that he was waking up to his mom asking if he would go clothes shopping with her. She said Mike needed to have some new clothes for school. Mike would rather be blown up with TNT than go to the mall to buy clothes. On the other hand, he did not want to have bad clothes for school. Many of his pants were too short and his t-shirts were dirty. He hated looking bad more than going to the mall. Especially since he knew that Ty, the school bully would just love to make fun of his worn out sweat pants. Unbelievably, when he went to shop for new clothes, he saw his friend Mark there too. Mark was at the mall with his mom buying new school clothes too. But they had no time to talk because Mike's mom was in a hurry because she was going to be on a conference call in an hour. So then Mike began picking out some new clothes for school at the Gap. He was surprised at the new larger sizes that he was wearing and that he was looking older. He brought the pile to the register and his mom paid with her charge card.

On the way back home they went through McDonald's drive through to get a soft serve ice cream cone. His mom did not have time to make him lunch so this was the only option.

They pulled in the driveway and saw Lilly with the babysitter on the driveway. Mike thought this was his chance to sneak in the house and get on the computer without his annoying little sister asking him a million questions. He quickly dashed inside and started his computer. He opened a single player game to get going on his ideas for new red stone machines. But his mom came in his room and announced that tomorrow was the first day of fifth grade. He needed to come down and eat dinner and then take a shower and go to bed early because he needed extra sleep for school tomorrow. He tried to argue with his mom telling her that he was not tired. He sadly ate his meatloaf and mashed potatoes and he fell asleep as soon as he crawled into bed.

Chapter 4

Before the first day of school every year, his mom takes tons of pictures of him in his new school clothes with his new backpack waiting for the school bus. This year he really felt embarrassed to have his mom taking so many pictures like he was a little kid. His school is Mayer Elementary School. This will be his last year there. His teacher is going to be Mrs. Notcher. She is the fifth grade teacher that everybody wishes they had. She was #1 very nice, #2 very patient and #3 very funny. Mark has her too this year. Last year they had different teachers and it was not a good year. Too bad Ty Kent was also in Mrs. Notcher's class this year too.

One word to describe Ty Kent was haughty. He thought he was far superior to everyone else in the fifth grade or in any grade and that everyone else was not as cool as he was. His parents were very rich and they gave him everything that he wanted. He always showing off all of the awesome stuff that he got from them at school. It made Mike feel sad that he could not have all of the things that Ty had. But Ty did not have any real friends. People just hung around him to get some of the awesome stuff that he had. Mike realized that fact in first grade when no one wanted Ty for secret Santa. The kids knew that Ty would just say whatever he got was "lame." Mike knew that Mark was a real friend of his and that made him feel better. But Ty was also a bully because he did not have friends. Mike had had several problems with Ty in school in the past. Like when Ty bragged about his new computer, he bragged about all of the tech specs on his new computer so much that Mike felt bad about his own computer. And when Mike made a report for extra credit, Ty said to the teacher that Mike had someone write it for him when he actually wrote it all for himself. Ty was just mean and Mike wished that Ty would just go to another school and bother someone else. Ty picks on Mike more than others because Ty knows that Mike knows a lot about technology. Ty was jealous and he wanted to make Mike feel like the information Mike knew was worthless. And one thing that he said is technology is for losers. Mike would need to be careful of Ty and do his best to avoid him and to keep his Minecraft ideas away from him. Mike knew that Ty would just make fun of them. This was very important to Mike.

Chapter 5

On the first day of school he and Mark were in class having fun doing their school work. The first thing they did was do part A of the vocab book. This year they were in the sixth grade book even though they were in fifth grade. Mrs. Notcher said that her kids were able to study well enough to ace the sixth grade book. If they had any problems with the higher vocab book, Mrs. Notcher would spend extra time with the student to help him to get back on track. That is the good thing about Mrs. Notcher. She wants to make sure all her students are prepared for middle school. Mike thought the book was a little hard but he could do it if he put in the extra effort. The fact that Mrs. Notcher thought that the kids could meet the challenge made Mike feel good about his chances of doing well in middle school.

After vocab, they had to read a book then write a book report about it. Mike read carefully and put in a lot of effort to write the report on the book. Mike and Mark were talking to each other about their reports and Mike looked away from it for a minute. Ty saw his chance to take the paper and mess it up. Ty scribbled all over it with a fat black sharpie and you could not read what was on it before. But when that happened, no one saw Ty do it. The teacher did not know what to do or who to believe so she said that Mike had to do it all over again. Mark had no problems at this point yet with Ty but when they were at recess Ty said "Are you friends with that loser Mike?" When Ty said that, a bunch of kids laughed with him because the kids just wanted Ty to like them so they could get some of Ty's stuff. This made Mark feel uncomfortable and he almost said, "NO." But then he realized that it would make Mike feel sad and so he just gave Ty a dirty look and walked away while the other kids giggled behind his back.

When they got in the lunchroom Mike and Mark sat right next to each other and tried to avoid Ty. When they got back in class Mike talked to the teacher about Ty Kent. He explained how Ty was a really big bully and told her some of the creepy things Ty has done in the past. Because the teacher was so nice she moved Mike's desk and Ty's desk to different sides of the class room. She also told him that she would try to stop Ty from doing bad stuff by talking to Ty's parents and telling them to discipline him. Mike did not know if that would help at all because Ty's parents were also not very good. They were bad news. Ty's dad would always yell at the umpires during summer baseball games. Ty's mom never smiled and never had anything nice to say to Ty that Mike had ever heard. Mike kept an open mind and hoped that this might just work. But he had a feeling that it might just not work. He had too much experience with Ty to believe that he would change just because Mrs. Notcher asked him to. The first day of school ended well except for that one unfortunate incident with the fat black Sharpie.

Chapter 6

On the bus ride home, Mike and Mark made plans to build a calculator in their Minecraft world later that evening. Mike got the idea from all the Youtube videos that he had watched the other day. One particular video showed how to make a simple calculator by using redstone and levers (which are also considered redstone.) Mike agreed to put it on the multi-player server on Mark's Mac. He wanted to have a reason later on to have Mark build something for him. He figured that if he built this where Mark could use it and take credit for it, Mark would help Mike later in building something else. They always had an awesome time making their plans for building new things in Minecraft. Mike is glad that school started again. Now he and Mark will be able to talk every day about Minecraft. He had many big plans for them.

As soon as Mike got off the bus and he went in the house, his mom asked him, "How was your first day of fifth grade?" He replies, "It was great except for Ty Kent. He was being very obnoxious and messed up my papers by writing all over them. I had to redo a whole paper because of him!" His mom says, "Are you okay?" He says, "Ya, I am. I did redo my paper and it was good. I just wish I would not have to deal with Ty." His mom asks, "Is there anything I can do to help?" To which he replies, "It is ok for now mom. I got it. I will let you know if there is anything that you can do later. I want to try to handle this myself. I don't want to give him anything to make fun of me for.. like having my mom fight my battles. But thanks for asking." She says, "I love you honey." He says, "I love you too mom."

After eating a snack of leftover pepperoni pizza with easy sauce and heavy cheese and chocolate lowfat milk, Mike ran up to his room to pound out his homework so that he could have time to play Minecraft with Mark later. His math packet was 65 pages long and he had to do 7 pages. It was on division. Mike had trouble with division. Division problems were complicated and they seemed to have too many steps. He often wished he could figure out an easier way to do it. But no, he never could but it was little fun trying to do things in a different way. He had more homework that was simple and soon he was all done.

He ran to his computer and called Mark. Mark was not home to answer his call. Mike was not happy because he was supposed to build the calculator tonight. As a solution, he logged into a single player world so that he could nail down the physics of the calculator to a science. The first thing that he did was make a display board. The display board showed digital numbers. It was made out of redstone lamps and stone for the background. The building was also made out of stone. It had buttons and signs above the buttons labeling them with the numbers that they would display. Right now he was working on the calculating part of it and trying to put it on a small enough place so that the game would render it out completely. It was important that all of the parts would load when he did all of the calculations. Once he finished the calculating mechanism, he moved on to bug fixing, otherwise known as debugging. One of the bugs was that whenever he did a problem that involved 8 and 9 it would get an answer that was completely wrong. He looked at the mechanisms for the 8 and the 9 and saw that the redstone crossed paths with each other for these two numbers. His solution was to make a bridge for the 8 over the 9 so they would not intersect. And it worked! But the problem was that the display board could only display three digit numbers. He expanded the display board by duplicating the display board that he had already made and then just added it on to the front of the board. This took him the rest of the night to accomplish. But when bedtime came, he was finished and he went to bed feeling like he had really done something that day. He was thinking of expanding the display board even more but he realized he was going to have to also modify the calculating part to accommodate the new improved larger display board. The basics would be the same. He would just have to extend the mechanism that converts the answer into digital numbers. "Wow, this is really turning out like a real life computer!" he thought as he was messing with the redstone in his head as he fell asleep.

Chapter 7

The rest of the first week of school was great, except for Ty. Mike continued to have problems with him. On Tuesday, Ty emptied Mike's water bottle into Mike's backpack when he wasn't looking. Luckily, even though his flash drive was in there, it was not damaged by the water or anything else and the drive still came out okay. But his lunch and snack were kind of weird to eat because they were soggy. On Wednesday, Ty started a rumor that Mike wet his pants. What really happened was Ty had put water on mike's chair to sit in and get wet. Mike found out it is hard to prove that you did not wet your pants . On Thursday, Ty hacked into Mike's Google docs account and saw a document from his personal journal and shared it with himself and then deleted it from Mike's account. Ty kept it in his account and then Ty sent it to everybody in his class except Mike. There were some thoughts in there about some of the teachers and his friends that he never meant for anyone else to see. Everyone was laughing at him and asking him why he said things like, "You think Mrs. Gars has a fat butt!" He couldn't figure out what had happened. He went on his account to find his personal journal to figure out how anyone could have known what he thought. He was surprised that he could not find the document at all. That was when he realized what had likely happened. Because Mike was good with technology he could figure out any password for all the kids' accounts in his school. He suspected it was something that Ty had done, so on Friday, Mike went into Ty's account first and searched for and found his personal journal. He shared it with himself and deleted from Ty's account and everyone else's account too. Once he had successfully stolen his work back, he did not know what to say because he was not supposed have all the passwords but he wanted to tell on Ty very badly. He decided to just not say a thing. He was relieved that he was able to delete it from everyone else's account. He hoped the other students just might forget what they had read and forget that the whole thing had ever happened. Ty was officially his nemesis.

Chapter 8

On the weekend, he did have fun with Mark playing Minecraft and basketball. One thing Mike was able to do on the multi-player server with Mark was to make the calculator work. But the thing they had to do was to build it there in the first place. By looking at his single player world, he made step by step instructions for himself to assemble it just as he had done there. It was very easy this time because he had a great understanding of how to build the calculator based on his previous work. Mark was very impressed with the result. Mike was also happy that he was obviously getting better. After it was fully built, they did some calculations on a calculator and it worked perfectly. They did calculations like 3 X 56 and 234 divided by 893 etc, complicated problems with not easy answers and they always got the right answer. No one else he knew had one, so he was very proud of himself.

Saturday night Mike's grandfather came over to see him and hang out with him while his parents took his little sister to a movie. They ordered pizza to be delivered with a 2 liter bottle of Grape Crush. Those were two of Mike's favorite things to eat. After dinner, Mike was wide awake but his grandfather fell asleep in the recliner. So he took advantage of that. He went on Youtube and watched a Minecraft "let's play" video. A "let's play" video is a recording of one player playing Minecraft usually on a single player game. The reason they record it and share it on Youtube is because there are plenty of people who want to see how other people play Minecraft. That way they can improve their playing strategies. Or they can do it just because it is fun.

So this night, Mike found a video by CaptainSparklez. CaptainSparklez is a famous Minecraft player. His real name is Jordan and he has his own Youtube Channel. He puts out a video almost every day. This video was on playing in survival mode and building a tree house. If you build a house in a tree, it is kind of cool. It also makes it easier on supplies because the tree provides shelter from Zombies. You just need to build a floor and build your bed there and place your chests in the tree. It is a lot easier than building the structure for your house. It keeps creepers and other bad things away from you because you climb vines to get up there and the bad guys cannot climb vines. They only problem is if an Enderman teleports to the top of your tree. Endermen can hurt you and they are pesky little fellows too because they walk around picking up certain blocks and putting them down in random places. Then you just have to rebuild what they took and get the blocks back from wherever they had placed them.

As CaptainSparklez built his tree house it became nighttime and it started raining in the game. Nighttime is when all the bad guys start to spawn. The rain at night with torches lighting the scene really made a dramatic effect. He was safe in his tree but it was really creepy. He did not know before that making a tree house was possible. He was glad CaptainSparklez put out these videos because they really improved his game play.

Shortly after the video was done, his grandpa woke up from his nap. Because his grandpa rarely comes to visit, Mike got off the computer and played checkers with him. They were almost done with the first game when his mom and dad and sister came home. They all had ice cream together and then he went to bed.

Chapter 9

Inspired by CaptainSparklez, the next day Mike started to wonder if he should make his own Youtube channel. After all, he was a good Minecraft player and good with technology, so he would be able to figure out how to make the videos. He thought of all of the cool things he could make and do. He thought about all of the kids that he could help with his ideas.

He began to make lists of ideas for videos he could make. These were some of his ideas: let's play episodes, redstone tutorials, small red stone machine descriptions, how to make a calculator, how to make a clock, different techniques for building train stations, how to make your own multiplayer server, tricks on finding resources, music parody videos using Minecraft animations, how to make a powerful TNT cannon, how to build a self-filling pool without dispensers, techniques for defeating the ender dragon, how to ride a gast, building and riding all types of roller coasters, how to survive your first night in Minecraft, how to install mods, making texture packs, reviews on different mods that he had already installed and used, how to make Endermen blow themselves up with TNT blocks.

These were just a few of the ideas that came to Mike's mind that day. Clearly this was something that he could really get into. He was pretty sure the subject would not get old to him. He was excited to share his ideas with Mark and ask him to help his new dream to come true. This was going to be epic if he could make it happen!

Chapter 10

The next day Mike went to Legoland Discovery Center with Mark and Mark's mom and sister. They enjoyed every part of it. The first part of the Discovery Center is known as Mini Land. Lego Master Builders spent hours and hours building a mini version of the city of Chicago. He saw all of the buildings in Chicago in their mini Lego form. And it was Star Wars week so there were all types of Star Wars mini figures placed all over the city. The Legoland employees put the mini figures anywhere they could. They did funny things with them like putting R2D2 rolling on top of a car. Darth Vader was riding a merry go round on its top and Luke Skywalker was lighting a car on fire. There were storm troopers everywhere, like dozens swimming in the water off of Navy Pier and many more riding in the boats in the harbor. There even was a storm trooper on one of the antennas on the Willis

Tower! It was like Star Wars wreaked chaos on Chicago.

Then when he had seen enough of this crazy madness, he went on to the next part of Legoland which was the Jungle. In the Jungle there were alligators, monkeys, and a hippopotamus all made out of Legos. Some of the Legos they used were Duplos, the bigger type of Legos. He thought it was amazing how many Legos they used there to make the animals.

On the Dragon Ride he then got to ride in a little cart that is supposed to look like a dragon. He was given a laser pointer that looked like a wooden gun but it was made out of plastic. You are supposed to shoot as many targets as you can or the bad guys that appear on the big screens along the path of the ride. When he got on he started to shoot the targets one by one and he was hitting many of them and so was his friend Mark. They loved the ride too. And then he got to the part when you had to shoot bad guys that were projected on a video screen. They then proceeded to the end where they supposedly save the dragon. He and Mark laughed and laughed as they shot their way through the tunnel.

After the dragon ride, they went upstairs to the Lego factory tour. They went there to see how Legos were made. They also knew they would get a free memento brick at the end of the tour. The tour guides always ask questions for the kids to answer like, "what are Legos made of?" Mike was the only one to ever answer "ABS Plastic", the tour guide said. They also asked more questions like how many colors does Lego make bricks out of. Mike thought it was 53 and he was right on that too! The factory always ends when the tour guide gives all of the kids a free yellow Duplo brick that says Legoland. Mike now has a collection of 7 of these bricks.

Mike loved going to the cafe at Legoland for lunch because the pizza was really great. They also always give you a free minifigure with each kids meal. Today he got a police officer minifigure. And cheese pizza. Mark got pizza too and firefighter minifigure.

After lunch they decided to take it easy by watching the movies. Legoland movies are all about Legos. The movies are all in 4D which means they blow wind on you and spray you with water and all that. They saw all three of the movies that they were interested in. Mike's favorite movie is Clutch Powers because it is just more exciting because of the action and the effects are really super 3D. Plus some of the movies do not have any spoken words just kind of like humming sounds made by the characters. Clutch Powers has real words and conversations. The other movies they saw were Spell Breaker and Lego Racers.

Following the movies, they went to the creative challenge area and had tons of fun building models of Pegasus. The Legoland employee wrote on the chalkboard that this challenge was to build a model from your own ideas of either a fairy or a Pegasus model. Since Mike and Mark were boys they decided to build the Pegasus model because fairies are for girls. It ended up that Mark won the challenge with first prize and all of the other people got prizes of Legos too. Mark got a yellow paper crown and no one else did. Mike was happy for his friend.

After the building challenge, they went over to the race track and built cars. They raced each other and Mike's car won. Then they both made modifications to their cars and tried again. Mike's modification was to make wings on the sides of his car to hold cars behind him so that they could not get in front of him. Mark's modification was to put more weight on it so that it would have more momentum. Then if a car got stuck in front of him, he would be able to crush it and push it out of the way since his was so heavy and big. They raced again and the problem was that Mike's car unstuck Mark's car. This pushed Mark's car across the finish line before his making Mark the winner. They high fived each other and both had a good laugh about that.

After about a hour of that, they went to the builder's workshop to build a Lego hamburger. Mark thought that a Lego hamburger was a funny idea. First of all they went in the door of the workshop and the guy who was telling them how to build it gave everyone a kit. They took their seats and watched the guy tell them how to build it step by step. The guy who was leading the workshop showed everyone how to do it by having a camera pointing at the model he was building and showing it on a TV screen. There were a few little kids that needed extra help and a the Legoland employee had to give them extra help and tell them what to do. At the end they each had a Lego hamburger! They both paid the $5 to take their models home because they liked them so much.

By then were getting tired and they had seen everything to be seen in Legoland . The retail shop is the last thing before you leave Legoland. It is positioned on the bottom floor right before the door. It has all types of Legos. It has pretty much all of the stuff a Lego store has but not everything. It has some things that the Lego store does not have too.

Mike and Mark had both wanted the Lego Minecraft set but they had not been able to buy it online because every time they were notified it was in stock, it sold out before they could order it. Most of the time is was within 3 hours of the email that they got that they were gone. They were for sale on ebay for $70 but they were supposed to cost $35! They were looking around at all of the stuff in the store when they looked up and saw a lady carrying Lego Minecraft sets to put on display to sell. They could not believe it! Mark took one as soon as the lady put it down and Mike soon followed and grabbed one too. They begged Mark's mom to buy them both a set. Mike's mom had given him some cash to spend but Mark's mom covered the rest. Mike and Mark both felt super-duper happy to finally own the Minecraft Lego that they both had been dying to get. The set was called Micro World and it had 480 pieces and most were 1 x 1 bricks or 1 x 1 square tiles. There were a few pieces that were bigger than that though. The coolest parts of the set to Mike were the Micromobs of Steve and the Creeper. Mike and Mark had gone as Steve and the Creeper for Halloween so they were really going to have fun with that.

Buying that set was the best part of the day!

Chapter 11

Mark's mom wanted to take them out for ice cream when they were done at Legoland. They chose to go to Red Mango. Everyone filled their bowls with yogurt and put tons of toppings on them. They weighed their bowls because that is how they are charged. Mark's mom paid for everyone. Mike likes vanilla with m and ms and Mark likes chocolate with gummy worms. Mike thought Mark's looked gross because it looked like worms in dirt.

On the way home they had to drop off Mark's sister at cheerleading practice which was fine with them because it gave them more time to talk about Minecraft. They were planning to make a clock that actually kept real time. Mike also started talking about his idea to start a Youtube channel with Mark and Mark loved the idea and said' "Let's go for it!" Mike was very glad to have someone like Mark to

share this with because it was just
better with a friend.

Chapter 12

This new idea was a big deal to the boys. The next day that they were at school, while Mike was talking to Mark about their YouTube channel, they were being very careful to avoid Ty Kent. They knew he would try and insult it and say mean things about it. Things like "You can't even play Minecraft well enough to cut down a tree, so how are you going to make a YouTube channel?" They did not want this to happen because all the kids would treat them badly and laugh at what Ty was saying. So the way they would talk about it was to hide on the playground under the slide. No one could hear them under there and no one could see them talking. It would be impossible for Ty to sneak up on them and eavesdrop because they could see him coming toward them. So they made a plan to have all their YouTube / Minecraft stuff on Mark's multi-player server. That way they both could see what

Mike was doing and Mark could give Mike suggestions on how he could improve his videos. Mark said, "Sure, maybe I could help you with your videos too. Maybe I could be a special guest so you could have someone to talk to and make it more interesting. The more the merrier!" Mike said, "Yes you can, I think that is a great idea. It will definitely help me to have your help when I need it. That will make my videos a lot more entertaining!" Right then, the whistle blew. And they did not talk about it while they were eating so that Ty could not eavesdrop.

Chapter 13

Ty knew they were planning something. Ty could tell they were up to something based on the fact that they were not talking. He asked his parents if they could get him professional grade listening devices. His parents said yes. They had tons of money and never said no to Ty. They did not even ask him what they needed them for! So he put those listening devices all over the playground. He put them anywhere he could think of because he had so many that he could do that. One day, the device that he planted on the slide got him the data that he was looking for. He found out what they were up to. So Mike and Mark were in trouble. He knew about their plans to make it big on Youtube. What Mike and Mark did not know was that Ty had planted the bugs. So they did not know that he knew about their plans. They were in trouble and did not even know it!

Ty started to make his own plans to sabotage and hack into their YouTube channel. His plan was to delete all the videos that they uploaded right after they get them up on YouTube. Because Mike and Mark talked about Mike's username and password one day, Ty's listening device caught that information. He wrote it down so that he could use it whenever he wanted to cause trouble. Ty felt really really happy now that he knew that he could do this to Mike and Mark. Even though Ty was walking around school like normal he felt even more superior inside than usual.

Chapter 14

The boys began to teach themselves how to record their Minecraft game. There is a program installed on the Mac called Quicktime Player. It makes it possible for a person to record what is happening on their screen and what they say. It does not necessarily show the person's face. It shows what is happening on the screen. It is a good tool to make the kind of videos that Mike and Mark were talking about making. They spent a lot of time playing around with Quicktime to figure out how to use all of its features. After making many mistakes and many failures and many Google searches for instructions, they finally figured it all out. They were ready to start getting material for their YouTube channel. This took them a couple of days. These were the days that Ty used to gather his information on them.

The boys continued to talk about their plans under the slide and Ty continued to hear what they were saying. He heard them discussing their plans for their first video. He was shocked and jealous of how much they knew. Their first video was going to be about how to get started in Minecraft. Ty thought it actually might be a big hit so he really did have to get rid of it. Because he was such a jealous guy, Ty had the idea to make his own YouTube channel by stealing the boys ideas. He could release his content before they could as well as deleting Mike and Mark's version before anyone could see it. He thought his plan was brilliant.

Unfortunately for Ty, Mike was very careful about security and changed his password but never did talk about it under the slide. He told Mark of the password change on the phone so Ty had no idea what it was. Ty had to change his plans. When he first saw the password was changed, he did not know what to do. He was confused because of this. He truly did not know what to do next. This was really disappointing to Ty. He had been so sure that his old plan was going to work. He formulated a new plan which was to ask his mom for money so that he could buy software that could hack into YouTube. The new plan was to view the passwords and user ids of the people who post videos. That way he would be able to get into their account even though Mike and Mark keep changing the password. He asked his mom to buy the software. Because they are rich and she is very busy she had her assistant go out and buy it. His mother did not even ask him a question about why he needed it except she did ask, "Do you need more than one copy?"

Chapter 15

One day at school, Mike found the device that Ty implanted into the slide.   Mike and Mark weren't happy about it. They knew that it could only be Ty who had done it. He was the only one who would have thought about doing this and the listening devices looked expensive too. The boys looked all over the playground by searching for black dots that look out of place. They carefully removed all of the devices so that Ty would not see. They were also careful not to damage them.

They were able to sell them to make money! Mark had a neighbor that likes this type of equipment and he does not like to shop in stores. They took them over to his house after school and offered to sell them to him.   The neighbor tested them first and they all passed his test. He gave them $300 for all of them.   The boys were really happy with the money.

When Ty came to get the data from the devices he did not know where they were. There were no devices to plug into his little tablet to get data from! He was not happy about that. He realized that the friends had stopped him again.

But Mike and Mark were happy because they were able to use the money to get new software that would help them make their YouTube videos. The software they bought was a graphics making program that would make it possible for them to make beautiful visuals for their YouTube videos. They had enough money left over to buy another program that allowed them to add special effects to their videos. This would help them to add in their own animations and have smooth effects. They took the new software to Mike's house and installed it on his computer. Then they did a test to explore the new programs they purchased. To give the new programs a trial run, they started a world and began recording what was on the screen. It was Mike walking around a Minecraft world as his character, Steve. They did that for about a minute. When that was done he ran it through his software. He was able to add a little design for their YouTube channel logo. The logo was animated frame by frame with their photo editing software. The video software that they used put all of those frames together so that it was one continuous animation. It was a little hard for Mike to do that. But when he was done it was worth the effort because it looked really professional. It was a Minecraft pixelated pick axe swinging side to side with their YouTube channel name "Two Boys One Minecraft" in background behind the swinging pick axes. They were going to have plenty of uses for their new software.

Chapter 16

Getting back to Ty and his new software... he did get Mike and Mark's password with it, but the problem was that the password was encrypted! That means that the letters that you see are not the actual letters of the password, so that left him stuck for the moment. He needed unencrypting software now. This kind of software works on most encrypted passwords, but not always. But Ty said, "I will give it a go, because my mom will give me anything I want. And I want this software!" So he went to his mom and asked for it. She commented, "You have been asking for a lot of software and technology related things lately. What are you up to Tyson?" His mom called him Tyson when she wanted to sound tough. Ty replied, "Oh, I have just been forgetting my passwords a lot lately. And this software just makes it easier for me mummy. Surely you understand." His mom remembering his other purchases too, "How do those listening devices you had me buy for you help you to get your passwords back?" He retorted, "Oh those? Those were a present for my Rex who is freak for spy equipment." His mom replied, "Oh that is good. I was just afraid you were trying to spy on me and daddy." "I would never think to do such a thing to my loving parents," said Ty. "In that case, I will have my assistant buy whatever you want as long as you can tell me why you need it," his mother said. "Of course Mummy." replied a very happy Ty.

Chapter 17

Ty's software came the next day delivered personally by Mrs. Kent's assistant. First thing he did was stick the disk in his disk drive. When he did that a little window popped up asking him if he would like to install it. He obviously said yes. It took about a half a minute for it to download. While it was downloading he was laughing an evil laugh to himself. He was tired of losing to those two losers! He was then prompted to finish installing which he also did. He opened it up to use it.

He tried to decode the password. The screen looked like a little window. It had a purple background with a bunch of buttons that said things like print, encode, and decode. There was also a little box which the user was supposed to paste your encoded password into. Then you click the button that says decode. He did that with Mike and Mark's password and it supposedly worked. He then logged on to YouTube and put the password in the YouTube login page but it did not work. He did not know that YouTube encrypts the passwords into a language that the program cannot decode!

Oh no, not again! Ty was mad because now he was locked out for real and there was really nothing he could do about it! He had to figure out another way to get the password. He thought and thought and realized that his best bet was to persuade Mark to tell him the password. He made a plan to try to trick Mark but Mark was not easily tricked. He saw through Ty's flattery and fake friendship and Mark said, "No, Ty are you nuts? Why would I ever betray my friend especially to someone like you?" At this point Ty realized that he had lost but maybe he might be able to get the password another time. He would just have to figure

out another way to sabotage their
YouTube channel.

Chapter 18

School work was getting to be challenging and more time consuming as the school year went on. Therefore they did not have a lot of time to make their YouTube channel. They were still able to develop their YouTube channel ideas but they did not have a lot of time to actually make the videos. It was not looking good for them through the month of November. But during Christmas break they had a ton of free time. They made their first video which featured Mike playing Minecraft single player in survival.

In this first episode Mike demonstrated how to make a proper tree house. It was a little like the CaptainSparklez video that Mike had watched only a little different because he had made a few improvements and practical changes.

Once he hit the ten minute mark he stopped and signed off. He put it through his new software to add their introduction logo. He brightened and darkened the film if he needed to for best picture for the viewers. When he was finished he watched the whole thing and he loved it! He immediately emailed a link to Mark in his Dropbox for him to watch too. Mark watched it and kept thinking that he could not believe that he was going to be part of this YouTube channel! Both boys realized that they were on to something great!

Chapter 19

Since Christmas break was so long, they decided to make one video each day for as many days as they could. That way they could stock up on footage so that they could upload lots of videos even if they did not have time to make them over the weekends during school.

The second video that they decided that Mike should record was a speed build of a model of the Willis Tower made with Minecraft blocks. Mike and Mark made an outline foundation for the Tower with Minecraft brick blocks. They needed to invite someone else on to their server because they needed someone to stand still in the game and record what they are building. The reason neither Mike nor Mark could record it was because they would be moving all over the place while they were building it and the recording would show that. So they needed one person to be in the game standing still and not building and recording what Mike and Mark were doing. Mark had a friend that had Minecraft that was good at technology too. He would be able to figure out the screen capture stuff no problem. His name was Joe. The 3 of them logged on to Mark's server and then positioned Joe in the right place for recording. Mike and Mark got to work building. They worked well together. It seemed liked they knew what each other were going to do and were able to work side by side.

The first thing they did was model the exterior. They used glass blocks and iron blocks to build the outside. It looked pretty realistic. Joe figured out the screen capture procedure and did it very well. Mike gave him good instructions and the recording was high quality. There were 30 interior floors and wood was made to separate them. They made a ladder-vator to get up and down. A ladder-vator was pretty much a ladder and a door to get out for each floor. It did not involve any red stone because it was just ladders and doors.

The build also used no mods. A mod is a modification for Minecraft. It is a program that is created to add stuff to Minecraft or change stuff that is already in the game. They are usually made by people who play Minecraft that are tech savvy. They know a lot about programming and want to improve their game to make it more fun. There is a great web site called Minecraft forums where you can find pretty much any mod that people have created and posted to share.

So when Mike got the footage back from Joe on the Willis Tower speed build that he and Mark built, he added his video intro to the video. He also fast-forwarded the footage so that the viewer would not need to watch it for hours and hours. Having done that, the building only took 15 minutes or so to watch it being built. It was cool to see it go up so fast. Once he was done he sent it to Mark. Mark loved it and so did Mike. Joe liked what Mike did to it and was happy that he was able to help with such a cool project. He was also proud to help someone who was going to be on YouTube. They were really learning a lot even though they were on Christmas break!

Chapter 20

Each video was getting easier. The next video he made was a video of how to make a big tree in Minecraft. Big trees look cool. The way he did that was to put 4 jungle saplings next to each other and made them grow. You make them grow faster immediately when you put bone meal on them or you can just wait. Mark decided to spawn in some bone meal since he was in creative mode to make the tree grow quickly.

As they grew, the saplings grew together and they made a 2 x 2 wide tree. Then Mike got rid of all the leaves by punching them and put dirt on the trunk of the tree that was left and put more saplings on the dirt. He placed the saplings in the same arrangement as he did for the original tree. They grew up fast because he added bone meal and then he had a double tree! Then he got rid of the leaves yet again and repeated the steps over and over again until he hit the height limit. He ended off the video after that. Then he put it in his movie making software and added the introduction to it. He looked at the video and noticed that there was no sound. He realized that he had forgotten to turn the microphone on so he videotaped it again this time making sure that he had turned it on. The boys continued to make videos all through Christmas break.

Chapter 21

Because both Mike and Mark loved roller coasters in real life, the next video they made was how to build a Minecraft roller coaster. Roller coasters in Minecraft are made with rails, mine carts and something to power the rails. Red stone torches usually power the rails but you could also use levers. Mike decided to use the redstone torches to power his track. He put down tracks and put down powered rails. Powered rails are different than track because they make your cart move and tracks do not. He dug tunnels through a mountain for the track to go through. When he got out the other side, he powered the track with redstone torches. You need to place a torch every so often to give it power. He made it loop back around to the starting point. He placed a cart on it and showed how you can ride your roller coaster in the cart. The tunnel that he dug through the mountain needed light so he also showed how to place torches in there. He felt pretty good about that video so he finished that one and edited the logo into it too. He was getting excited now that he had 3 complete videos for making his own YouTube channel. His goal was to make seven complete videos before the end of Christmas break and he was doing great at meeting his target.

The ideas were coming together nicely and they were working as a team. For the next one, Mark thought it would be cool to make a music video using note blocks in Minecraft. A note block is a block that when it gets supplied energy by redstone current it produces a sound. You can hook them together to make a musical song. Each note block makes one sound so you have to put lots of these blocks down together to make a song. This was more like a note block song than a tutorial but it took a lot of time and effort to get the song right. They made up their own song too so it was completely original. When you watched it, the video looked like someone running around a bunch of red stone and note blocks. They did not video the building of the note blocks into the song, they videoed the song playing after it was built. They were proud of their work and really enjoyed watching their song play. It was a great melody that made them feel happy inside because it was very cheerful.

Chapter 22

Because of a debate that he read in a thread in the Minecraft Forums, the next video Mike and Mark made was how to build a self-filling pool that did not involve dispensers. Dispensers can dispense water that can fill up the pool if you have enough of them. The uncool thing about that is that you need to refill the dispensers. They can only hold nine water source blocks so you have to refill them constantly every time that you fill the pool which is very hard.

Having a self-filling pool that does not need a dispenser is very useful. Mark thought it would make a good video and that kids would want to learn how to do it. Mark adapted the idea from Ethoslab, a well-known YouTuber, and his way of filling a giant square of water quickly without having to place down every single source block.

The way Mark built his pool was he dug a hole in the shape of a square. It has to be a square for it to work. He placed two lines of diagonal barriers made of birch wood planks, but you can use anything. He liked the way the birch wood looked. He then placed source blocks of water in between the barriers. Then all he had to do was remove the barrier blocks and the water would fill the whole pool. But he decided to cover up one end of it so that there would not be a walkway in the middle of his pool. He used sticky pistons to pull back the block so that the water could creep out to fill the pool and then they could push back the blocks when it was filled. It only takes a couple of seconds to fill.

It was a brilliant plan and in the video he thanked Ethoslab for the inspiration.

Chapter 23

Since a lot of Mark's friends were asking him how he installed a mod called "Too many items" he thought this next video should be "How to install too many items". The video began with Mark going into his bin folder in the Minecraft config file. Once he was there, he looked for a file called Minecraft.jar. In that file was everything that is used to configure your Minecraft game. At this point he had to make the Minecraft jar into a zip file. Then when he unzipped the zipped folder, he got a folder not a jar file of everything that Minecraft runs off of. This way he could actually go in and edit his Minecraft.

He looked for a folder with the title of "Meta-inf" and deleted it immediately. If you do not do this once you edit your Minecraft, your game will be black and rendered useless. As you can see this was a very important part of the tutorial.

Once this was done he pasted all of the contents of "too many items" which he had downloaded from Minecraft forums into the configuration file for Minecraft. He had to highlight everything in that config file and compress it. When he finished compressing it, he had to search his Minecraft configuration folder for something called archive.zip that appears when you compress a file. He dragged that out into his bin folder and renamed it Minecraft.jar and threw away the old Minecraft.jar. The last step is that he closed the Finder window and opened up Minecraft and opened up one of his worlds and showed the viewers that he had successfully installed "too many items."

Too Many Items is cool because it is like having creative inventory in survival mode with a couple of perks. The perks are being able to change the time, turning rain on or off and even changing game modes in the middle of a game. That is why everyone wants this mod. And now everyone can install it easily if they do watch Mark's video. He was excited to get this out on the web because a lot of people were requesting this.

Chapter 24

Since he loves playing with TNT in Minecraft, his next video was about fun things that you can do with TNT. TNT is a block that is crafted by using gun powder. Gun powder can be obtained from creepers when you kill them. Or you can also kill a ghast to get some but the problem with that is ghasts also drop ghast tears. Ghast tears are used to brew certain potions and they drop ghast tears more often than they drop gun powder so you have a better chance of getting gun powder from killing a creeper. The other thing about it is that ghasts are pretty hard to kill.

You take your gun powder and mix it with sand at your crafting table and then you get TNT. TNT is pretty fun to play with. You can use it for mining and a lot of other things, like TNT cannons. Mike decided to use this show to demonstrate how to make a TNT cannon. He made the TNT cannon out of obsidian just in case it blew up. Obsidian has the quality of not blowing up unless you can somehow put 285 TNT blocks right on top of it.

The cannon he built was a compact creation on top of a pretty hill. It used TNT to propel the TNT out of the cannon. The player would press a button and light the starter TNT and it will explode propelling the next TNT block out of the cannon. The flying TNT block will explode a little later. If TNT is shot in a way to have the TNT block explode in midair, it will look like white fireworks. If you put fewer repeaters on the TNT block that will be fired, it will explode more quickly giving it less of a chance to hit the ground before it explodes. A repeater is something that slows down the redstone signal that causes the TNT to explode. Redstone current stops after 15 blocks, so you need to place a repeater to keep redstone current moving. The cannon he made was able to shoot TNT a good 75 blocks high in the air. The explosions looked like a white sparkling spray of particles. It was fun to fire that off a couple of times. What guy does not like to make things explode? He knew this would be a popular show because people like Minecraft TNT.

Chapter 25

He wrapped up his video making with one last video. In this one he would show beginners basic mining techniques. The first thing he demonstrated was the need for building stairs down to where you are going. If you do not make stairs, and you dig straight down, you will not be able to get back up. Another problem is that you might dig straight down into lava. So digging down and sideways is a better idea. That way you can see what is coming up and you do not kill yourself. Mark showed exactly how to build a staircase down to the level that you want to mine resources from. On his way down he was lucky to find a vein of diamonds to show the viewer how to mine along the way down. He explained that you need an iron pickaxe or higher level pickaxe to mine diamonds. Then he dug down to an area that had a lot of redstone and was excited to tell his viewers that you need a diamond pickaxe to mine redstone. Lucky for him he had all of these types of pickaxes in his inventory. This was really going well.

As he dug down more he found an abandoned mine shaft. You can randomly find these mine shafts underground. The only way to come across one is by digging around. He explained that you can find random chests sometimes lying around while you are digging. These chests have resources in them that you can take and add to your inventory. He was lucky to find one that had melon seeds in it to show how you could get lots of resources underground. He explained how to open a chest by right clicking on it, super easy.

Chapter 26

The next day was Christmas so he was really excited about that because he had a lot of technology items on his Christmas list. He wanted a disk burning machine, a new microphone, a two terabyte hard drive, and a cardboard Minecraft Steve head. He unwrapped all of his presents quickly. One of them was a disk-burning machine and some disks. He was very happy that it came with 25 disks too because then he could start burning his videos onto the disks. That would make it easy for him to give them to Mark so that he has a copy too. The videos would be too big to email so this will really help.

The second present that he opened looked very very square. He thought and hoped that it would be the cardboard Steve head and by golly he was right. He put it on right away so that his mom could take some cool pictures of him opening up the rest of his presents wearing it.

He had five more presents left to open but he only asked for four in total. He was surprised. His mom surprised him by being way cooler that he thought she could be by ordering him an Antvenom t-shirt. Antvenom is a guy on YouTube that plays Minecraft and makes good Minecraft videos to post on his channel. The t-shirt was black with white words and Mike loved it. He took off his pajama top and put on the Antvenom t-shirt with his Steve head. Then he turned back to his presents.

The next box was small and heavy for its size. He was not sure what this was going to be. It ended up being a one terabyte hard drive because his parents did not want to spend the extra money on a two terabyte drive and they thought one terabyte was huge and was good for now.

There were three presents left. He hoped one of them was going to be the microphone. The next box he picked up was lightweight and he had no idea what it might be. He was thrilled when he opened the box and saw that it was a wireless number pad for his wireless keyboard. A number pad actually helps you scroll through items in Minecraft inventory by clicking the numbers and then you can go to specific items without having to page through them. He never could understand why the wireless Mac keyboard did not come with a number pad. The wired keyboard has one.

He shook the next box and heard a bit of rattling. It made him think of Legos. So when he opened it, he saw a preassembled Lego camera and also some Legos to customize it. His parents must have found this on eBay because he had never seen one in the Lego store.

There was one box left. It was his last chance for getting a microphone. He grabbed the paper and ripped it off and underneath it was a box that said USB microphone! It was the snowball microphone. It was just what he wanted!! This Christmas was spectacular because he got a lot of stuff. It was also great because he was on his way to having his own YouTube channel.

Chapter 27

After Mike's family was done opening their gifts, they went to his older cousin's house who also liked computers and Minecraft. Once they were there and had said hello to everyone, Mike tried to get some computer time with his cousin. His cousin's name was Adam. Adam was 17 years old and was always willing to teach his younger cousins stuff on Minecraft and computers. He was a real nice guy too.

Today Adam wanted to show Mike how to make a piston doorway. So he first showed him what it looked like when it was built on his server and then he showed him how to build it himself step by step. The first thing that they did was put down all of the sticky pistons. A sticky piston is a piston that holds on to a block and does not just push it. The sticky pistons have blocks built on top of them and to their sides. They also have blocks to push. After that he laid down the red stone which made the sticky pistons turn on or off, meaning push or retract. The button was an important next step because otherwise it would not activate. The button was placed over the arch of the machine. When pushed it triggers all of the blocks to push each other and the blocks to hide the doorway. They were done building with that step. They played around with it and built a house that used that same doorway as an entrance to get in and out of. Mike also thought that this would make a great YouTube video.

Chapter 28

Once Mike got back to school from Christmas break Ty bragged a lot about all the stuff he got from Santa. But he was still missing something... Mike and Mark's password! He thought about it all Christmas break. He needed to either stop them from having an awesome YouTube channel or he needed to have a more awesome YouTube channel than them. But since he did not like to work that hard and he like wrecking things, getting their password was the best idea for him.

He kept thinking about how he could persuade Mark into giving him the password. Ty was able to trick him by saying, "Hey what did you want this Christmas and did not get?" Mark replied, "A basketball signed by Kobe Bryant." Ty said "What if I were able to get that for you if you were to do one favor for me?" Mark said "What favor?" Ty replied "Give me Mike's password for his YouTube account." Mark said "Sounds like a good deal to me." But only because he would tell Mike to back up his video files so that nothing Ty did would matter and nothing bad would happen. So Mike did. Good thing he got that 1 Terabyte hard drive for Christmas!

Mark gave Ty the password with a smile. So Mark got the basketball. Then Mark told Mike to change the password tomorrow. Ty was able to log in to Mike's account and he was so proud of himself. He was so proud of himself that he actually forgot to delete the movie files or even look at them. He figured he could always go back and do whatever he wanted. So Mark got the basketball and the password only worked for one day.

Ty tried to log back in the next day and was unsuccessful and did not know what happened. When he got to school he went looking for Mark. Ty asked Mark what had happened. Mark said "I have no idea," even though he knew that the password was changed. He did not tell Ty for fear that he would persist in bothering him to get the real password. Ty thought that there was something weird about his Internet so he tried again the next day but still it did not work.

It was driving Ty nuts because Mike was walking around school telling everyone about his videos that he had made over Christmas break. Ty had his chance. He had them right where he wanted them but did not delete anything when he had the chance. He was really upset about that. What he did not realize was that even if he did delete them Mike and Mark had a backup of the videos to repost. Ty realized that he was going to have to actually make his own awesome channel to compete with Mike and Mark since he was not succeeding at cheating to win this battle.

Chapter 29

Before Mike and Mark were going to actually launch their YouTube channel, they wanted to be ready with several episodes of Minecraft "let's play" on their multi player server. So during January they worked on those in their spare time either after school or on the weekends. They went like this...

The first "let's play" episode showed them trying to build a tree house together. The first thing they did was get up to the top of the tree. They needed vines to do that. And the vines were not growing fast enough so they tried another tree and that tree was just right. They climbed up the tree using the vines that had already grown up on it. Also they had to break off some of the leaves because they grow on the trunk.

When they were at the top of the tree, they began construction. They did this by replacing the top layer of leaves on the tree with wooden planks for the floor. They then put down their crafting table, their chests, their furnaces and their beds. They put up one block tall walls around the outside of their house. And then they explained to the viewers that there was an option of building a ceiling and they proceeded to show their viewers how to do it. They built a little column up to where they wanted their ceiling to be. Then they built out from their column to make it cover their whole place. Once that was finished, they could demolish the column because in Minecraft blocks can actually float! They finished off this episode with Mark killing a pig and eating pork chops to celebrate their new house.

Chapter 30

The next episode featured the making of tools to go mining for resources and rarities, like diamonds, iron, coal and gold to make better tools. Also, while they were mining for these they were trying to find lava. That was important because you could pour water over the lava to make obsidian.

Obsidian is important because you can make a nether portal out of it and because obsidian does not blow up as discussed before. After you put water on top of the lava, you use a diamond pickaxe to mine out the obsidian. With this, you can make a nether portal with the obsidian block that is horizontal and is 6 X 4 blocks tall and wide. Then you spark the middle of your portal with flint and steel to make a block inside the portal. When you touch it you will find yourself in the nether! Mark and Mike were hoping to go to the nether one day in their survival series.

Chapter 31

They were getting very efficient at making videos. This night, they actually were able to make a second one. This next episode showed them mining away and making torches by right clicking on the crafting table. They explained that they were selecting a piece of coal from their inventory and crafting it by putting it on top of a stick to make a torch. If there is not enough light, bad creatures can spawn. So players like to place torches down so bad creatures would not spawn where they have been. Because they still could spawn in the places that players did not put down torches, they were careful to have swords on them so that they could fight off monsters. They found lots of coal and some iron.

They were digging deeper to find more rare resources like diamond, gold and maybe emeralds which were 25 times rarer than diamonds in Minecraft. They suddenly heard some hissing sound from right behind them. That could mean that there was a creeper near. TNT makes that hissing too, but that would not make any sense for it to be what was making the sound now. They pulled out their swords and quickly started looking for the creeper. Soon they both saw it and started to swing their swords at it. Sadly, they were not quick enough. It exploded and it almost killed Mike. His heart bar went down to two hearts and full health is ten hearts. The explosion actually mined out some iron for them which they quickly gathered up. Mike ate some pork chops that he had in his inventory, to restore his health.

When he was at full health again, the two of them started to get back to mining again. They were digging along when they dug themselves into an abandoned mine shaft. This is really good luck because the tunnels in them are dug out already and they also have chests randomly placed. Chests almost always have valuables in them. Two things that are normally in the chests are pumpkin seeds and melon seeds. You can plant these to grow pumpkins and melons which are a pretty good food sources. So they were glad when they stumbled upon the mine shaft. They looked around it first for any chests that they could see. They found one around a corner down a dead end. They opened it up and got all of the stuff. This one had five pumpkin seeds and three melon seeds plus a bonus three bones, which can later be converted into nine bone meal. The bone meal makes your seeds grow immediately. It is like super fertilizer. This video was going really well. Mike thought that if he was watching it, he would love it.

Then next thing that happened was they explored the mine shaft further and they found preplaced cobble stone that could only mean one thing. There was a dungeon built here that had a mob spawner in it that could spawn all sorts of bad guys like creepers, skeletons and zombies. They did not run the other way because they knew there would be a chest in there that had good stuff in it. Once the light gets bright enough on a mob spawner, it stops spawning bad guys. They explained what they had to do. They put torches all around the mob spawner so that it was so bright that no bad guys could spawn. Then they safely took the loot from the chest and mined the chest itself because they needed the chest so they do not have to make one with their own resources. That is recycling Minecraft style.

As they got deeper into the mine, they ran out of torches and had to craft some more. Mark and Mike kept on mining until Mark ran into a vein of some diamonds! After he mined the diamonds, he told Mike that he would make some diamond pickaxes - one for each of them to mine resources faster and just to get certain resources.

Near the end of the mine shaft, there was a lava pit running through it. When Mike found the lava, he put water on top of the lava and made obsidian and mined it with his new diamond pickaxe from Mark. He got so much obsidian that he pretty much had to make an enchantment table and nether portal with it. He crafted the enchantment table down in the mine and then sprinted to the surface and placed it down on their tree house.

He then went back down to the mine and continued mining. He found tons of coal and iron so he made iron swords for the both of them. He went back to where he found the lava and kept on mining near it. He was lucky and found a lot of redstone blocks and mined them too.

He told Mark about his find so that he would start brainstorming some possible redstone creations. He came up with a machine that would protect their tree house by killing monsters that walked near their tree house. The system used pressure plates to shoot arrows like crazy toward any bad guys that got close to their house. The problem with that is that he had to remember that they were there when he came back home. He had to remember to jump over the arrows to not get shot by his own arrows and killed. He thought he could do that and he made sure that Mike was aware of it too.

This was a pretty long video. They ended off by luring a creeper into their trap and having it get killed by arrows. They collected the gun powder and ended off the episode. Mike was really excited about their creeper killer episode and was really beginning to believe that they would have a successful YouTube channel. Now that he was positive that they would have good content, it was time to start uploading their videos to YouTube.

Chapter 32

They went to YouTube and signed in and uploaded their first video with plans to release a new video each week. He also included an audio portion to the video. He hoped that "Two Boys, One Minecraft" would become a hit.

The very next day at school, kids started coming up to him saying things like, "Nice job, Craft," and, "Mike, I like your style." Not tons, but enough to let Mike know that he was onto something good. Ty noticed too and was extremely jealous. He had not made any videos yet and still did not have the password, so there was little he could do to compete or take down their YouTube channel. So, all he could do was walk around saying that their video was not very interesting and that they would not last long. He hoped that he was right. But he had a bad feeling that this was going to be better for Mike than he had thought it would be.

He began to make other plans and try to get new ideas to ruin Mike's success.

His first idea was to try to get all of the kids in school to stop liking Minecraft. Since so many kids hung around him, he began to tell them that he was over Minecraft. Now he was now totally into Dragonvale. He hoped that everyone would stop playing Minecraft and then stop watching Mike's videos if they got into a different game. He walked around school with his iPad showing everyone the cool new dragons he was breeding. It half worked. There were some kids that listened to him but there also were many who just loved Minecraft and did not care what Ty said about Dragonvale. They tried it out and then went back to Minecraft. He was getting really frustrated because he hated it when someone had something that he did not have. And Mike was going to do

that by having a real YouTube
channel with subscribers galore.

Chapter 33

Mike did get into Dragonvale a little too but he still liked Minecraft better. He figured out that Ty was trying to undermine his YouTube channel by saying bad things about Minecraft. He was thinking of starting to make some Dragonvale videos which would totally negate Ty's plan to make people stop watching his videos. Having Dragonvale videos might even help him get more viewers on his YouTube channel. Maybe they could even get some of the kids that Ty was tricking to watch. Ty promoted Dragonvale so much that there were many kids were getting into Dragonvale. This might just work out for Mike anyway. It actually made him kind of happy when he realized that Ty was trying to stop people from watching his videos.

To help teach kids about Dragonvale, he started his Dragonvale game over again so he could show his park developing. He also showed the viewers how to breed dragons. His first dragon to breed was a lava dragon and he told the viewers how to breed it. Soon he was getting to the point when you would need to start breeding epic dragons. He got prepared for hatching them by purchasing the habitats for those epic dragons in the Market. He got his first epic dragon and it was the moon dragon! The moon is cool looking and it has a very cool habitat. It looks like the moon and the dragon lives on top of the moon in its habitat. The next dragon he was trying to breed was an opposite dragon called the blue fire. An opposite dragon is a dragon that contains 2 opposite elements like cold and fire. You can do that by breeding a hybrid that contains one of the elements with the other element. After it hatches, that dragon makes a lot of money too.

Between those two dragons he was able to make a lot of money for a starter. He had clever strategies. He thought he could get a lot of views. When Mike got back to school, he told Mark about it. Mike also said to him to not tell Ty or else he might find a new way to bully Mike. They agreed to keep it as quiet as they could but they realized as soon as they posted their first Dragonvale video that Ty would find out.

That night Mike went home and put his first Dragonvale video on his Two Boys One Minecraft channel. They got about 125 views the first night! This really proved that his channel was catching on with viewers. They got many likes too and they were starting to get subscribers as well. It turns out that a lot of kids who play Minecraft also get into Dragonvale or wanted to find out more about it. This was a very good thing for Mike. Not so good for Ty. Mike felt like thanking Ty for the idea,

but he figured Ty would just get mad and do something crazy.
Chapter 33

As Mike and Mark kept posting their Dragonvale videos in between their Minecraft videos, their popularity at school soared. Ty however was in a very bad mood. He had accidentally given Mike and Mark the opportunity to improve their channel. Ty hated that. It made him crazy with jealousy. He promised himself he would find a way to get back at Mike and Mark for making him look stupid by becoming so popular. He just did not have a plan yet. He would have one soon because this was the only thing he was thinking about now.

All together they have gotten 9,000 views after only 2 weeks and one new video was posting every four days. They would have liked to do them more frequently but they did not have that much time to record content and get new ideas. It was very helpful to have Dragonvale videos to post too because that gave them fresh content and time to think of new ideas for their Minecraft videos. As it was, they were using up their Christmas break videos quickly and having little time to record new ones.

Chapter 34

School was fun but busy. The science fair was coming up and Mike needed to make a science project. The idea he came up with was to have a bunch of experiments using water to demonstrate different principles in physics. There would be two main ones. One was a bowl of water that you could drop things in to observe the water surface and see how surface tension keeps the water in the bowl. Then you could put a drop of soap in the bowl and see how it breaks the surface tension. The soap causes all of the water to spill on to the tray on the table. The second demonstration had to do with inertia and friction. The way that worked was he filled a small cup with water and put it on to a paper napkin. Then he quickly pulled out the paper napkin from under it. The cup barely moved! He explained that if you would pull it out slower, it would have fallen off of the table and made a big mess. That was because of inertia. Inertia explains what he did because the first law of motion says that a body at rest tends to stay at rest unless acted upon by a force like friction. Since he pulled very quickly, the friction did not act upon the cup very much. The other kids thought his display was cool. Kids love it when water can potentially spill all over the place. Plus these two experiments looked like magic.

Ty, of course, said to all of his fake friends, that Mike's display was lame. Ty had a giant volcano that his dad's butler built for him. It looked very realistic and it actually looked like it exploded. As a joke he had a picture of a Dragonvale lava dragon next to his volcano, but not so close that the fake lava would damage it. Mike's little sister was afraid of it because it was so big and Ty had rigged it with his iPad to make rumbling noises when it exploded. It was very obvious to all of the kids that

Ty had not done the work. However they could not prove it. The teachers gave Ty the first place award and Mike came in second. He congratulated Ty on his win and was pleased with own prize.

All of the planning for the science fair had taken up a lot of time over the past couple weeks for both Mike and Ty. Ty had not tried anything with the password problem and Mike had not made any new videos. Now it was time for both of them to get back to work.

Chapter 35

Ty went back to the spy equipment store and bought some spy gear that would record keystrokes on a keyboard. He thought that he could figure out the password that way if he could just install the gear on Mike's keyboard. It was actually software-based so Ty tricked Mike into giving away his computer IP to him by sending him a fake email. The email looked like it came from a website that Mike had visited for computers. Now that Ty had Mike's IP address he remotely installed the spyware onto Mike's computer. He thought this was really going to be great. He spent days monitoring Mike's keystrokes but could not understand why Mike was typing all kinds of things like grocery lists, chore calendars and emails to all of the moms at school. Then he realized that Mike had given out his mom's IP address not Mike's personal computer's IP address.

He was stopped again. He could not believe it!

While Ty was wasting his time watching Mike's mom's key strokes, Mike was busy making new videos for Two Boys One Minecraft. The Minecraft videos were definitely more popular than the Dragonvale ones, but he still made some of those too. He made more Minecraft than Dragonvale.

The next episode he did for Minecraft was one about fire arrows. Fire arrows are arrows that get shot through lava. There is one other way to shoot fire arrows too. He showed the viewers both. The way to do it without lava is to enchant a bow with fire aspect. When you enchant a bow it is not certain what enchantment you will get. So he explained that you may have to enchant a lot of bows. He did not want to have to do that so he showed how to use the mod "too many items" to enchant his bow to make sure that it became a fire bow. Once he had shown how to do this, he also showed how to use lava to make the arrow to go on fire. He did this by putting dispensers behind lava that is flowing down from above then shooting arrows through the lava. This makes that arrows burst into flames and then the target the arrows hit will also start to burn. This is useful to kill animals and get cooked meat for your inventory. At the end of the episode he spawned a creeper in front of the firing arrows and the end of the show was the creeper dying before he could explode. This was getting easy for Mike and he looked forward to doing more.

Chapter 36

Somehow the video he made on TNT cannons over Christmas break had gotten corrupted. He wanted to make another TNT cannon episode for his next video. The first thing he did was make his base, which was 3 X 6 X 2, out of obsidian, so it would not explode if anything went bad. He dug out a 1 X 4 X 1 hole on the top and middle of the TNT cannon. He put redstone on one of the sides of the TNT cannon all the way down the 5 blocks. The reason he did that is so the ammo at the front of the TNT cannon did not get triggered. He put a button to control the redstone next to the redstone that he just laid down. Then he put a different button right next to the ammo TNT to control the ammo for the TNT cannon. He labeled them to make sure it was clear which was which. He put the TNT into place. He remembered to get rid of the first TNT and replace it with water to make sure that the TNT that is used to shoot the ammo does not do any damage to the land. He pressed the first button and then the second button and watched. He saw a big BOOM! He also explained that you could extend the back of the TNT cannon. He showed his viewers how to do this by just building out the original design a couple of blocks. A longer TNT cannon is just a little more powerful he explained. That was the end of that video. Mike then saved it and showed it to Mark. Mark said, "I cannot wait to make that TNT cannon myself!" This video was even better than the first one he had made. He was almost glad he redid it because he was getting smoother with each video he made.

Chapter 37

As weeks went on, Mike and Mark were becoming like rock stars at school and Ty was feeling very bad. The YouTube channel was a big success. They were getting many likes and subscribers. The comments they were getting were like "Dudes you rock," and "I love your videos," and "Can't wait for your next video!" This really made Ty move into action. He actually started to make his own videos. He watched all of the videos that Mike had made and posted and took his ideas and just copied them. Mike was better at Minecraft than Ty was, but Ty managed to pull off making some pretty decent videos just because Mike's ideas had been so good to begin with. His channel was called Minecraft Man and he also started to get some views. When kids at school asked him why he was into Minecraft again, he just said that if Mike can have a successful channel with Minecraft, I want one too. He then said if Mike could do it even a baby could do it. He began to make videos every night after school and he was able to start posting them pretty regularly. The comments that Ty started to get did not make him happy. Kids were saying he was just a copycat and that he should not try to be "Two Boys, One Minecraft" which really blew his top.

Then his videos started to turn mean. He began to make fun of Mike's YouTube channel in his episodes. Pretty soon his videos started to be as bad as he was. There were not many people who wanted to see that kind of thing. Ty's views went down to almost nothing.

Meanwhile Mike and Mark kept making quality Minecraft videos and just ignored Ty because they thought he sounded crazy and that no one would listen to him.

Chapter 38

Mike and Mark started to build a hardcore adventure map to share with their viewers. A map is a pre-built Minecraft world that someone makes and shares in the Minecraft forums or any other way the builder of the map wants to distribute it. They thought it would bring more viewers to their channel and have other people play their adventure map so that they would advertise their YouTube at the same time. They began by brainstorming ideas of what they would like to have in their map. They came up with the idea to name their map The Ocelot Jungle. The main part of it was a temple that was full of jungle stuff, like trees and ocelots. This was different from a jungle temple which naturally spawns. They had to build this temple and fill it with jungle stuff for the players to explore.

One unusual thing that they made in it was that they put a bunch of creepers in there. Ocelots kill creepers by whamming into them repeatedly until the creeper dies. The ocelots destroyed them in a minute. The player who entered the jungle temple did not know that that was going to happen. The player would run and run and run from the creepers but the ocelots helped the player not get killed.

The map did have challenges for the players to try to complete, like taming 20 ocelots. For that challenge they made it easy because they gave you a fishing rod and a pond. Ocelots like to eat raw fish. So you went fishing for fish to feed the ocelots and tame them and make them your friends in a way. The map was pretty much a free for all. You could go anywhere you wanted that was in the boundaries. There were challenges that you were supposed to do any way you could think of.

For example, there are many ways to train ocelots. But there were certain challenges that you were contained in a set boundary that there was only one way to do it.

Mike and Mark did not know how to put rules into the game. Mike thought that he could make a book with the rules, or maybe use signs or command blocks. Because Mike liked redstone he made a command block system. He made a button that triggered the command block sequence. He programmed them then hooked them up and tested it and liked it! Then they built some of the challenges and wired them with redstone to make them more challenging and complex. They included a special cave and placed the resources themselves for the players to find. They dug a hole in the ground removing everything that was there then covered their fake cave with a layer of bedrock all inside of the cave too. They did that so that in survival mode there would be no way out.

This made them think of an idea that they should put bedrock under the first layer of grass. That way the player could not escape or find resources that they were not intended to find. They carefully placed the resources that they intended them to find.   Where there were no resources, they put a layer of stone so that it looked more like a cave and not a bedrock shack with randomly placed resources. Their entire temple was made out of bedrock so the player could not escape.   That way the player knew exactly where they were supposed to stay and not stray outside of the boundaries. Also, if a player found out a way to dig through the bedrock, Mike and Mark put a layer of lava. Then if they dug through the bedrock, the lava would kill them.

The main challenge for the players of this map was a lava jumping challenge. There was a giant lake of lava that had a path of pillars for the player to leap across. If they fell, they died. The point of this challenge was to get to the other side of the lake to complete the challenge without falling at all. Mike and Mark both tried it and failed many times before they got it.

There were a few more cool things that they added to their map like a bowling alley that used ice and clay blocks. When you throw the clay block, it gets on the ice and keeps going until it falls in a hole. This triggers a pressure plate that makes the map know that you have finished the challenge. They also made a mansion for the player to live in when it was night time so the bad guys would not kill them. It was a three floor mansion including a finished basement. The bedrooms were on the top floor. They had the kitchen room which really only had cake on top of a wooden block on the normal floor.

There were paintings, fake furniture and an enchantment room/ brewing room and a swimming pool that was made with their self-filling design. The outside was decorated with flower pots full of flowers, cacti and all different types of saplings. The gardens were very pretty. The outside of the building was made out of brick blocks. The inside was made out of wood for the floor and the walls.

They made a big creeper out of wool. It was a big statue that looked like a real creeper. They made it have flashing eyes with red stone. They also made a challenge in the creeper too. It was a challenge to complete a red stone circuit. The way it worked was there was a redstone path but there were spots that you needed to have a sticky piston that pushes the block to finish the circuit. The trick was that some of the pistons have already pushed the block where it was supposed to be. So if they just went around flipping levers, they would not correctly complete the challenge. It was very important that they be careful. The boys tested it out and it worked if you were careful.

Chapter 39

The next thing to do was to get a Minecraft Forums account. They set it up under the "Two Boys, One Minecraft" name. They got their account but they still needed a Media Fire account. After they got that account they were able to upload their map and used that link on their Minecraft Forums thread. To help promote their new map, Mike then videoed himself playing the map. He sent the video to Mark. Mark approved the video and he also tested the map to make sure it was playable for people besides Mike.

They posted the video of their map on their YouTube account and put the link to that video on their forum thread. They also placed a link to their map on the video page. Over the next week, they watched their progress by seeing how many hits their channel was getting. They also watched how many subscribers signed up. It was fantastic! Other people started checking out the Minecraft forums page too. After this addition, people started making their own reviews on the map. It was cool to know that a lot of people liked their map. This also blew up their views on YouTube.

They were getting so many views that YouTube contacted them about setting up a contract where they would get paid by the number of views. When Mike got that letter, he could not believe it. They were officially a big success. They were going to make money by doing what they loved! This was the best day. Mike ran to call Mark. Mark was so excited that he swallowed his gum. Their parents all came running to see why they were both yelling. Their sisters were happy too. They were kind of famous for real. This was what they had worked so hard for. It was worth it.

Chapter 40

When they got to school the next day, they shared their big news with their teacher, Mrs. Notcher. She had known about their channel but did not understand much about it before they told her. But she understood that this was really a big deal. She made the announcement to the class that Mike and Mark were YouTube celebrities and that they would be busy over the summer making new videos and posting them. Since it was May and the weather was nice she gave them a second recess to celebrate. Ty was so jealous that he stayed in the bathroom and would not go out to celebrate. That was just fine with Mike and Mark because Ty would just try to ruin it somehow if he was on the playground.

While Ty was in the bathroom he was trying to think of a way to turn this around and he was coming up blank. If he tried to say they were stupid, he might look stupid since they were a real success and making money on YouTube. He knew that would not work. He was beginning to think that they had won.

Out on the playground every kid that was out there came up to them and congratulated them. A few of them even asked for their autographs. Mike even signed some using his Captain Craft name. This was a lot of fun.

Both Mike and Mark realized that they could not just stop here. They had many more ideas for their Minecraft careers.

Chapter 41

They needed to make Minecraft mods and texture packs. They did not know what mod to make or what texture pack to make at first. Mike thought that they should make a texture pack that made glow stone not look so bad. Also he thought of another mod to make glass easier to see through. Mark thought their mod should be a house bomb. The house bomb was a block that when you place the bomb down you put a lever near it. When you flip the lever, it will look like it is exploding but when it explodes it actually builds a house. The problem was this had been made already. So Mike made it look like a black hole spitting out blocks to make a house which has not been made before. The blocks were hopefully going to spin when they got out of the bomb. But when they landed in their position they would stop spinning. A different feature Mark wanted was for the blocks to build from the roof down because the bomb was going to be set off on the ground it would look like blocks were magically coming from the ground into the air.

The first thing he worked on was the bomb itself. He made the texture for the bomb. Next he needed to make the house design then he made it magically appear when you trigger the bomb. The problem was that Mike needed to make the house in code. Mike had started learning from YouTube video tutorials how to put certain block formations into code. So coding was Mike's job and Mark's job was testing and offering suggestions. Mike got back to coding after watching those videos and put the block formation into code. Mark tested it and it worked but there was a problem. It simply did not look as magical as they had wanted it to. It was good though. Except for the fact that Mike did not put a chest, furnace, crafting table and bed in the house and

Mark pointed that out. Mike then put those into the code. Mark set of the bomb again and it made a fully functional house! Mark set it off in a village so a bunch of villagers started to swarm it. That was funny.

Now they had to work on making it look magical. He needed to figure out how to code animations. He looked at videos on animating blocks so that they would spin around. The animation he learned was able to do this. So he did it. The problem was the blocks did not build the house. They stayed spinning on top of his house bomb. That was not good.

He had to figure out how to make a pathing code to make them move to where they needed to be. He did that by watching tutorials too. Next he needed to figure out how to make them stop spinning once they got into position. He did that by watching tutorials on stopping animations. After all that video watching and learning, he did it. The house bomb was almost ready. Now he just wanted to make it build from the top down instead of just all at once flying out of the bomb. He accomplished that by putting a delay on each layer from the top down making the bottom layers appear last. That was really cool. Mark tested it and it was exactly like they wanted it to be. The only thing Mark had suggested was to make it spawn a basement. Mike said, "Maybe in a few updates." With their mod completed, they moved on to their texture pack.

Chapter 42

The plain glowstone block in Minecraft looked kind of ugly to Mike and Mark. They thought that changing the colors and the outside pattern on it would help. They thought glow stone should be yellow with a circle made with a thin line of black in the center of each block. Mike did this by getting a picture out of his Minecraft folder called terrain.png which had all of the blocks before they were folded up into their 3D form. He looked for the glow stone texture and edited it the way he wanted it. He went in and did the same for the glass blocks and made them more invisible. So that you still noticed that they were there, he put a blue dot in each corner of the glass. Now they had a texture pack too!

They needed to make their texture pack compatible with their mod. So they added the texture of their bomb into the terrain.png picture.

They were sure to also leave a copy of the original terrain.png picture for those people who did not install their mod and just installed the texture pack.

Now that they were done with their mod and their texture packs, they put them on the Minecraft forum under their account name. Anyone who wanted them could use them! Having this stuff on the Minecraft forums and being able to show it on their YouTube videos would help their channel become more popular as people used their creations and left positive reviews for them.

Ty would leave negative reviews sometimes. But other reviewers would leave posts saying Ty was nuts and that Mike and Mark's stuff was great. Mike was getting so popular at school that kids were calling him Captain Craft instead Mike. It made Ty pretty mad when he heard that. Mike and Mark were getting used to being more popular than Ty and they liked not having to worry about him. They knew that they had that popularity for a good reason not a bad reason. It was almost as good as not having Ty in school at all.

Chapter 43

The school year was winding down. It was June already. This year had gone very quickly. Fifth grade was Mike and Mark's favorite year so far. They had done well in school and had made something that would help them in life. They had a YouTube channel that was starting to make them some money. Kids listened to them and had stopped listening to Ty and had stopped thinking he was funny. Ty was acting like he was going crazy. Mike felt bad about that but he could not feel too bad because Ty deserved what was coming to him.

Mike and Mark began to plan what else they would do with their new business this summer. Mike knew a little computer programming including some HTML so that he could build the "Two Boys, One Minecraft" website. They wanted to include links to all of their past videos so that people could always get to them. They also wanted to include links to every texture pack and mod they produced.

The biggest thing that they wanted their web site for was to have "Two Boys, One Minecraft" and "Captain Craft" merchandise. Mike's mom knew some people who could help him with that. She also knew where to get t-shirts, sweatshirts and bobble heads made for them too- and at a good price. This was actually becoming a good family activity. For everyone except Lilly that is. She still just messed things up. Luckily, he now knew how to keep his cables safe from his little sister.

The got the domain name for twoboysoneminecraft.com and started to design the t-shirt that they would sell. They wanted the t-shirts to be in a variety of colors with black and white made in the largest quantities. Mike designed the graphics using Adobe Illustrator. He used the 3D text tool in Illustrator to make the images to go on the t-shirt. They had three main designs. One was a picture of two Steves with the words, "Two Boys One Minecraft" in 3D above them. The second design they had for the t-shirts was a picture of their TNT cannon that they had shown how to build in one of their videos. The final one had a picture of Captain Craft's skin holding a block of TNT. That one really made Mike laugh. He had a prototype made and wore it to school on the last day of school. Kids ran up to him and told him that it was cool. He gave them his web address and told them they could buy one too. He explained it would probably take him a week to get his web site up so they would need to check in a week.

His last day of fifth grade was turning out really well. His teacher gave him the Hardest Worker Award which made him very proud. He really felt like he was a hard worker and he liked that he got that award. He also won the Most Likely to Succeed Bill Gates award because he was so good with technology. Mark won the Best Friend Award since he was nice to everyone in the class. Mike really agreed with that one. Mark also won the Most Likely to Be a Professional Athlete award. Mark was thrilled with that one.

All of the kids were wondering where Ty was that day. The last day of school is always the most fun day of school so you would have to be really sick to not be there. The word started to get around school that Ty's parents had pulled him out of Mayer Elementary and put him in a fancy boarding school for middle school. That made it official. This was the best year ever!

Printed in Great Britain
by Amazon.co.uk, Ltd.,
Marston Gate.